Fancy NANCY

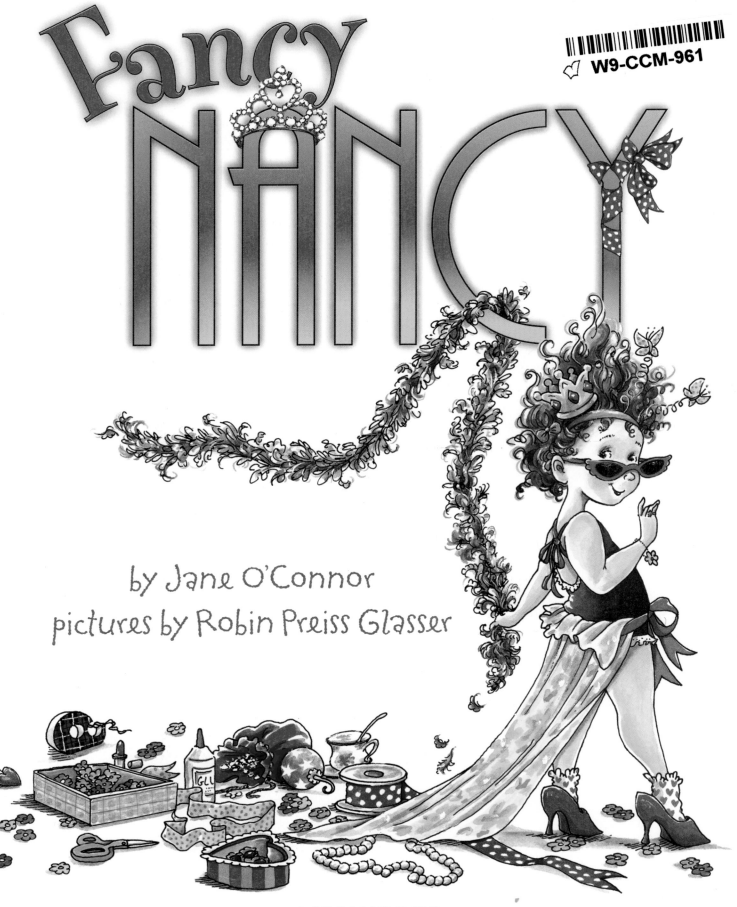

by Jane O'Connor

pictures by Robin Preiss Glasser

SCHOLASTIC INC.

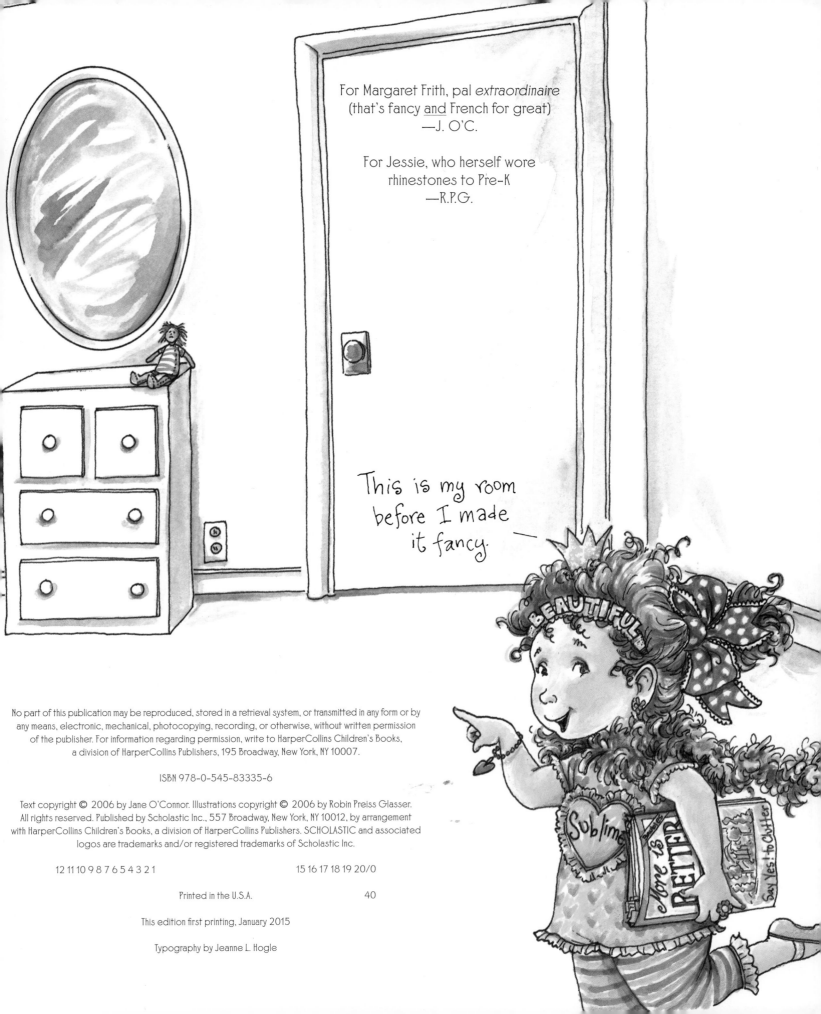

For Margaret Frith, pal *extraordinaire*
(that's fancy <u>and</u> French for great)
—J. O'C.

For Jessie, who herself wore
rhinestones to Pre-K
—R.P.G.

This is my room
before I made
it fancy.

ISBN 978-0-545-83335-6

Text copyright © 2006 by Jane O'Connor. Illustrations copyright © 2006 by Robin Preiss Glasser. All rights reserved. Published by Scholastic Inc., 557 Broadway, New York, NY 10012, by arrangement with HarperCollins Children's Books, a division of HarperCollins Publishers. SCHOLASTIC and associated logos are trademarks and/or registered trademarks of Scholastic Inc.

12 11 10 9 8 7 6 5 4 3 2 1   15 16 17 18 19 20/0

Printed in the U.S.A.   40

This edition first printing, January 2015

Typography by Jeanne L. Hogle

I love being fancy.

My favorite color is fuchsia.
That's a fancy way of saying purple.

I like to write my name with a pen that has a plume.
That's a fancy way of saying feather.
And I can't wait to learn French because *everything* in French sounds fancy.

Nobody in my family is fancy at all.
They never even ask for sprinkles.

There's a lot they don't understand....

Lace-trimmed socks *do* help me to play soccer better.

Sandwiches *definitely* taste better when you stick in frilly toothpicks.

A princess is supposed to keep her tiara on.

"What's a fancy girl to do?" I ask my doll, Marabelle. Her full name is Marabelle Lavinia Chandelier.

Then I get an idea that is stupendous.
That's a fancy word for great.

Maybe I can teach my family how to be fancy.
I make an ad and stick it on the fridge.

Plain	Fancy
Yellow	Gold
Leather	Patent leather
Glasses	Sun glasses

Marabell

Fancy

Plain

Plain

Fancy

walk for the cure

Fancy

Plain

Fancy Stuf

Soon there is a knock on my door.
My family saw the ad. They want to get
started right away.

The trouble is, my family doesn't own any fancy clothes.

That's okay. I go find—what is that fancy word?
Oh, yes!—some accessories.

Ooo-la-la! My family is posh!
That's a fancy word for fancy.

My mom twirls in front of the mirror.
"Why don't we go somewhere fancy tonight?"

"How about dinner at The King's Crown?" Dad suggests.
Wow! My parents are acting fancier already.

"May I escort you lovely ladies outside?
The limousine is waiting."

My dad is our chauffeur.
That's a fancy word for driver.

When we arrive at The King's Crown,
everyone looks up.
They probably think we're movie stars.

"For dessert, let's have *parfaits*," my mom says.
"That's French for ice-cream sundaes."

Amazing! My mother knows French!

When our parfaits are ready,
I curtsy and say, "Merci."

I carry the tray like a fancy waiter.

Oops! I trip. I slip.

The tray does
a double flip!

I don't feel fancy anymore.

I want to go home.

After I get all cleaned up, I put on my dressing gown.
Those are fancy words for bathrobe.
I feel much better. I'm ready for a parfait.

I tell my parents, "Thank you for being fancy tonight."

"I love you," my dad says.
"I love you," my mom says.

And all I say back is, "I love you."
Because there isn't a fancy—or better—way of saying that.